MW01096731

Midnight
A Cinderella Alphabet

by

Stephanie Perkal

Illustrated by

Spencer Alston Bartsch

To my dear friend Sarah Miller, Happy reading!

Stephanie Perkal 10/2/99

Shen's Books

For my mother and father,
who gave me endless books as a child,
and endless encouragement as an adult.
- S. P.

For my parents,
and Branden, my little reader.
- S. A. B.

Shen's Books 821 South First Avenue Arcadia, CA 91006
http://www.shens.com
Printed in South Korea.
Text type is Korinna.
Display type is Bellevue.
The illustrations were first drawn by hand and then
scanned into a computer and rendered.

*Shen's Books publishes books for children and young people
that affirm universal values.*

The author & illustrator would like to gratefully acknowledge the following
people for their generous contribution to this book: Gary Frenkiel,
Dr. Sylvia Kennedy, Dr. Adrianna Kezar, Kathleen Kopta, Maywan Krach,
Julie Perkal, Jane Priewe, Nancy Rose and Janet Wong.

First Edition

1 2 3 4 5 6 7 8 9 10

Library of Congress Cataloging-in-Publication Data

Perkal, Stephanie, 1967-
Midnight : a Cinderella alphabet / by Stephanie Perkal ; illustrated by Spencer Alston Bartsch.
-- 1st ed.   [32] p. 31 cm.
Summary: Using a word for each letter of the alphabet, a grandmother introduces her two
grandchildren to the many versions of Cinderella told around the world.
ISBN 1-885008-05-8
1. Cinderella (Tale)--Juvenile literature. [1. English language--Alphabet--Juvenile literature.
2. Cinderella (Tale) 3. Fairy tales. 4. Folklore. 5. Alphabet.] I. Bartsch, Spencer Alston,
1960-   ill. II. Title.
PZ8.P417Mi 1997   398.2--dc20   [E]   96-38241   CIP   AC

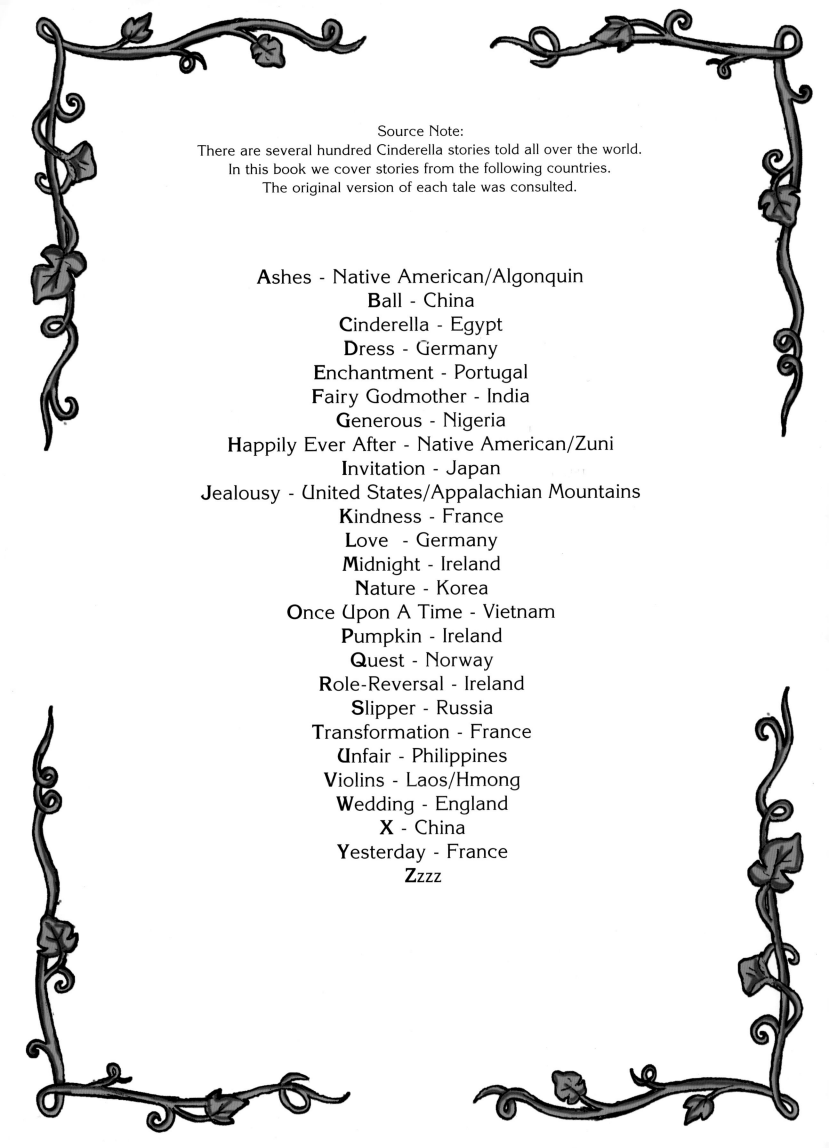

Source Note:
There are several hundred Cinderella stories told all over the world.
In this book we cover stories from the following countries.
The original version of each tale was consulted.

Ashes - Native American/Algonquin
Ball - China
Cinderella - Egypt
Dress - Germany
Enchantment - Portugal
Fairy Godmother - India
Generous - Nigeria
Happily Ever After - Native American/Zuni
Invitation - Japan
Jealousy - United States/Appalachian Mountains
Kindness - France
Love - Germany
Midnight - Ireland
Nature - Korea
Once Upon A Time - Vietnam
Pumpkin - Ireland
Quest - Norway
Role-Reversal - Ireland
Slipper - Russia
Transformation - France
Unfair - Philippines
Violins - Laos/Hmong
Wedding - England
X - China
Yesterday - France
Zzzz

"Well, children, I believe it's time for you to go to sleep."

"Oh, Grandma," cried Millicent. "Will you tell us the Cinderella story?"

"Again? I tell you that story every time you spend the night."

"Please?" Matthew asked. "And can we have a piece of pumpkin pie?"

Grandma chuckled. "Of course. I made it just for you. You know I can do wonders with a pumpkin. Now, about that story. Cinderella...hmm. Where would you like me to begin?"

"Once upon a time, Grandma," Millicent said.

"Alright, dear," Grandma replied. "Once upon a time, there was a kind and lovely young girl named Ella. After her mother died, her father married a woman who had two daughters."

"And they were very mean to Ella, weren't they?" Millicent asked.

"Yes, Millie, they were," Grandma continued. "While Ella's father was away they were quite mean and made her do all the chores and sleep by the fireplace. That is how she got the name Cinderella, you see, sleeping near the ashes and cinders. One day..."

"A footman came from the castle with an invitation to a royal ball!" Matthew cried.

"That's right, dear. Cinderella wanted to go to the royal ball more than anything, but her stepmother would not allow it. After Cinderella helped her stepsisters dress for the ball, she was left behind to clean up after them. Cinderella was so sad and lonely that she sat down by the hearth and began to weep."

"And then her fairy godmother appeared!" Millicent exclaimed.

"And she turned a pumpkin into a coach and mice into horses!" Matthew mumbled. His mouth was full of pie.

"Yes, children. Isn't that wonderful? The fairy godmother granted Cinderella's wish. Cinderella's ragged dress magically became a beautiful ball gown, and glass slippers appeared on her tiny feet. The fairy godmother was careful to warn Cinderella to leave the ball before the clock struck midnight. When Cinderella arrived at the ball no one recognized her, not even her stepmother or stepsisters. Everyone thought she was a princess from a far-off land."

"And the prince danced every dance with her, didn't he?" Millicent remembered.

"This is a yucky part," Matthew added.

"Yes, the prince did dance every dance with Cinderella. But when the hands on the clock approached midnight, Cinderella had to rush away. She did not want to disobey her godmother. As she ran down a flight of stairs..."

"Her glass slipper fell off!" Millicent interrupted. "And the prince picked it up and said he would marry the girl who left it behind."

"Another yucky part," Matthew groaned.

Grandma continued, "Cinderella was very excited when the prince came to her house while searching throughout the land for the girl whose foot fit the glass slipper. Cinderella's stepsisters each tried to put on the slipper, but their feet were far too large. Finally, it was Cinderella's turn..."

"And the slipper fit!" Millicent cried.

"Yes, it did," Grandma agreed. "Then her fairy godmother appeared and once again turned Cinderella's ragged dress into a lovely gown. The prince recognized her and knew he had found his true love at last."

Millicent smiled.

Matthew yawned and asked for another piece of pie.

"Instead of another piece of pie, why don't I tell you some more Cinderella stories?"

"Are there more?" Millicent asked.

"Oh, yes. People all over the world tell Cinderella stories. The story we know comes from France. Why don't you climb into your beds and I'll share some other versions with you."

The children ran down the hall and jumped into their beds.

Grandma sat down on a comfortable chair. "Perhaps one day you can share these tales with your own grandchildren. They are as easy to learn as A, B, C..."

A ashes

Cinderella sleeps next to the fireplace and gets dirty from the ashes. There is a Native American tale about a maiden who is somewhat like our French Cinderella. This poor girl's face has been scarred by burning cinders from the fire her mean sisters force her to tend. A great invisible hunter is the only person in the village who can see beyond her soot-covered face. He sees her true inner beauty.

ball

Charming Cinderella meets her prince at the royal ball. It is said that long ago, in ancient China, the very first Cinderella story was written. This story does not have a royal ball. It has a cave festival. Yeh-shien, the Chinese Cinderella, wanted to attend the cave festival, but was stopped by her stepmother. Magic fish bones came to her rescue and granted her a special wish.

C Cinderella

In many countries, Cinderella has a different name. The ancient Egyptians called her Rhodopis. Rhodopis was gathering reeds by a river one day when a great falcon swooped down and snatched up one of her sandals. The falcon flew straight to the pharaoh's palace and dropped the sandal in his lap!

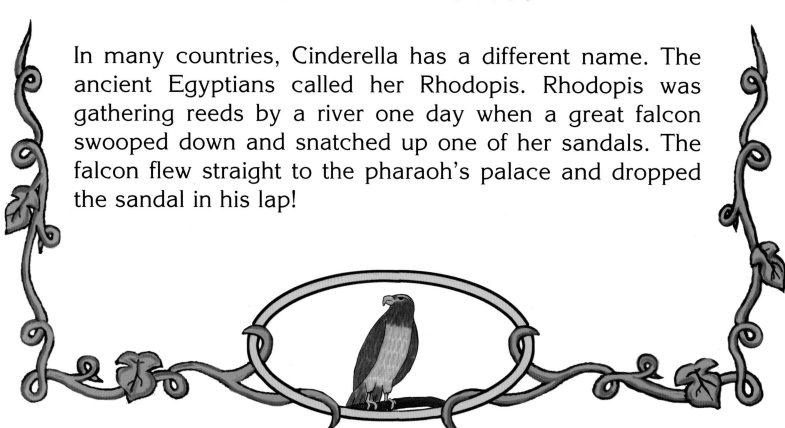

dress

Cinderella's dress is ragged and torn until her fairy godmother turns it into a ball gown. A German Cinderella story tells of a princess who has many special clothes. She wears a cloak made from the fur of a thousand animals and has three magnificent dresses which are as golden as the sun, as silver as the moon, and as sparkling as the stars.

ℰ *enchantment*

Magic turns mice into horses and a pumpkin into a coach. There is even more enchantment in a story from Portugal. It tells about a prince who is turned into a fish. A lonely girl finds the fish in a pond and decides to keep it as a pet. The fish falls in love with the girl and asks for her hand in marriage. When she surprisingly agrees, the fish turns back into a prince. Her vow of love has set him free.

 *fairy godmother*

The fairy godmother uses magic to help Cinderella find true love. In a tale from India, a spell-binding snake helps a young cowherd find his true love. The snake turns the cowherd's hair into gold, and a princess finds a shining strand of it floating in a river. When the cowherd and princess finally meet, the snake promises them a happy life together.

G

generous

Not only is Cinderella hardworking and patient, she is also kind and generous. A girl in a tale from Nigeria is so giving, she shares what little she has with a hungry frog. The frog repays her with a beautiful dress, elegant jewels, and dainty shoes to wear to a village festival.

H happily ever after

The prince and Cinderella live happily ever after, but the Zuni Cinderella does not have a happy ending. It is the tale of a maiden who tends a flock of turkeys. Because she is kind to the turkeys they reward her with a doeskin dress and beaded jewelry to wear to the Dance of the Sacred Bird. The maiden breaks her promise and stays too long at the dance. When she finally returns to her flock, they have all flown away.

I invitation

Cinderella is invited to the ball, but her stepmother will not let her go. In a Japanese version of Cinderella, a girl is invited to a play. Her stepmother forbids her to go until her many difficult chores are done. When she eventually arrives at the play, a great nobleman is captivated by her beauty and falls in love with her.

J *jealousy*

Cinderella's stepsisters are envious of her beauty. A tale from the Appalachian mountains is very similar. Two sisters are so jealous of their housemaid's beauty that they not only force her to wear dirty clothes and sleep next to the fireplace, they even hide her under a washtub when visitors come!

$\mathcal{K}$ *kindness*

Cinderella often shows her worth through acts of kindness. In another French story, the prince gives Cinderella a gift of oranges and lemons, which were rare and costly at that time. Even though Cinderella's stepsisters have always been cruel to her, she is kind enough to share her precious oranges and lemons with them.

L

love

The prince finds his true love with the help of a slipper. A prince in a German story finds his true love with the help of a gold ring. He gives the ring to a princess after dancing all night with her. The next evening she disguises herself as a kitchen maid and serves him his dinner. Imagine his surprise when he sees the ring on her finger!

M midnight

Cinderella has to leave the ball by the stroke of midnight. One of the Cinderella tales from Ireland has a different kind of deadline. A prince must rescue a princess before the third tide rolls in. An evil sister of the princess tries to keep the prince from saving her. Fortunately, the prince is able to save the princess just before a whale swallows her.

$\mathcal{N}$ *nature*

Nature is often Cinderella's only friend. A story from Korea tells of a girl who must work while her lazy stepmother and stepsisters watch from nearby. Animals come to her aid and help her to finish some difficult tasks. A black ox helps her weed the dry rice fields and a gigantic frog plugs up a hole in her water jug.

O once upon a time

Cinderella's troubles begin when her father marries an evil woman. Tam, a Vietnamese Cinderella, shares the same fate. She becomes so sad and lonesome after her father marries a selfish woman that a kind-hearted spirit comes to her rescue. Some people believe that this is the same spirit that helped the Chinese Cinderella.

pumpkin

Cinderella goes to the ball in a coach made from a pumpkin. In another Cinderella story from Ireland, an old woman gives a young girl three magical horses to ride to church. At the church, the girl meets a prince who is charmed by her beauty. When she refuses to tell him who she is, the prince pulls a shoe from her foot.

Q quest

After the prince loses Cinderella, his quest is to find her again. A story from Norway tells of a prince who has an unusual idea of how to meet a mysterious girl. He spreads sticky tar all over the ground around the girl's horse. When she tries to ride away, she finds her horse stuck in the tar!

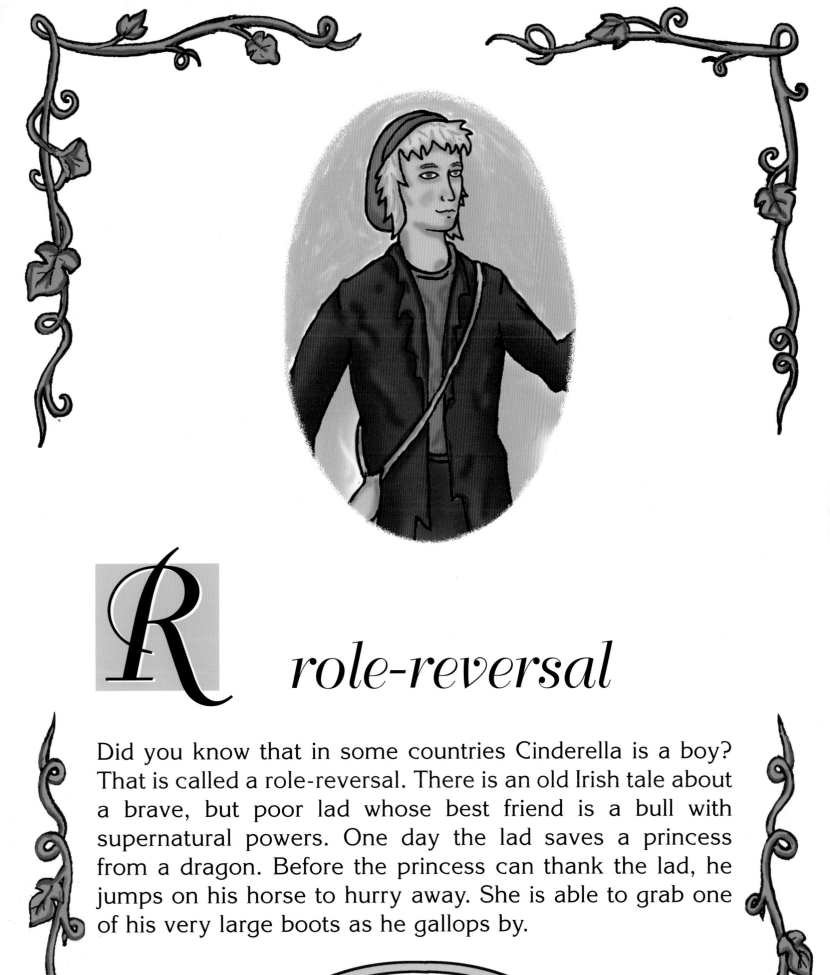

R role-reversal

Did you know that in some countries Cinderella is a boy? That is called a role-reversal. There is an old Irish tale about a brave, but poor lad whose best friend is a bull with supernatural powers. One day the lad saves a princess from a dragon. Before the princess can thank the lad, he jumps on his horse to hurry away. She is able to grab one of his very large boots as he gallops by.

S *slipper*

In many Cinderella stories it is the slipper, left behind in haste, which brings two people together. In a tale from Russia, it is beautifully woven linen that allows a girl to meet her true love, the Tsar. A magic doll left by the girl's mother helps her to spin thread and weave fabric. The cloth is so delicate and special, it is fit only for the royal Tsar.

T transformation

Cinderella's rags are changed into a beautiful evening gown by her fairy godmother. An unusual French story is just the opposite. It tells of a princess who runs away from home. She visits a wise old woman who gives her a donkey skin cloak to wear as a disguise. When she puts the dirty cloak over her noble dress, she is so transformed that no one recognizes her.

U

unfair

Cinderella is treated badly by her family. A Philippine Cinderella story tells of a girl whose scheming stepmother makes her bathe in a river filled with crocodiles. When an old crocodile splashes water on the girl, a drop lands on her forehead. It turns into a radiant jewel which dazzles everyone, including the king, who falls in love with her.

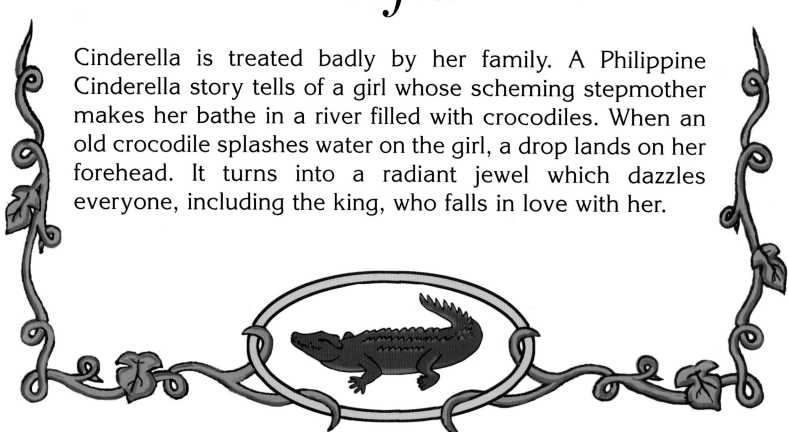

violins

Cinderella and the prince dance to the romantic music of violins. A Cinderella story from Laos tells of a kind, but mistreated, Hmong girl who meets the son of a village elder during a New Year celebration. They play a game of ball toss and he grows very fond of her. That evening he serenades her with songs from his bamboo flute.

W wedding

True love is united when Cinderella marries the prince. In an English story, a wealthy girl meets a young nobleman after her father disowns her. In this tale, the young man actually becomes ill with love for the girl. The only remedy for him is to marry her. Later, they have a grand wedding, and she is reunited with her father.

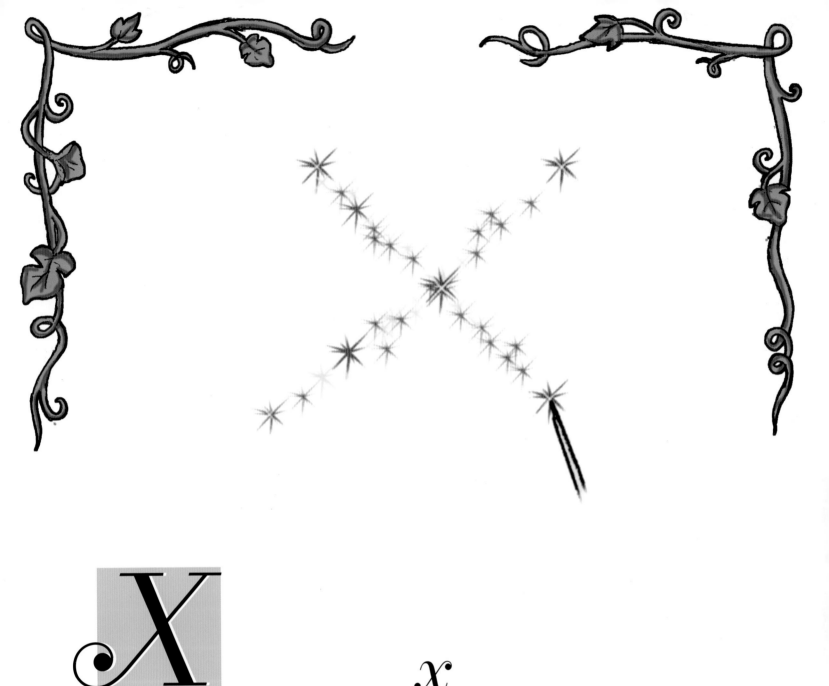

X x

The fairy godmother's magic wand crosses over Cinderella and transforms her. Yeh-shien, the Chinese Cinderella, does not have a magic wand. She does have special fish bones. Because she treats the bones with respect, they grant her wish for an emerald-green gown and golden shoes to wear to the cave festival.

yesterday

In our French story, and in many others, Cinderella forgives her family for their past cruelty. Yesterday is completely forgotten. She now looks forward to a happy future with the prince. Cinderella invites her family to live with her in the castle and even arranges for her stepsisters to marry lords of the court!

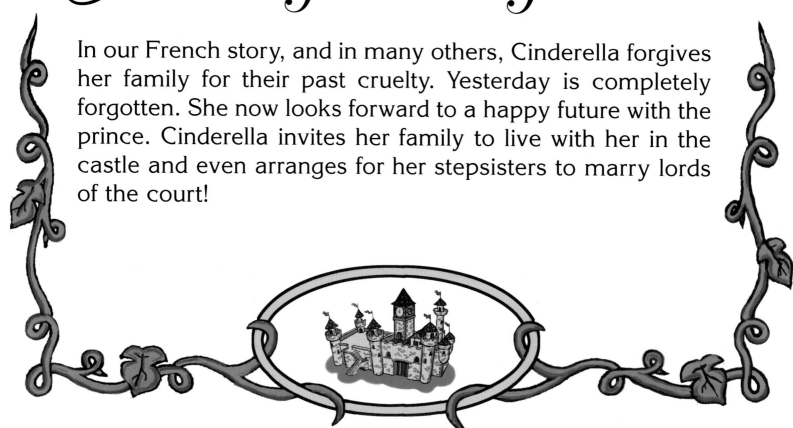

Z

ZZZZZ...

Oh dear. It's almost midnight and long past your bedtime.
I've had such a nice evening sharing these stories with you.
Sweet dreams, children. And remember...

...your fairy godmother is always here for you.